Praise for VERITAS

"Truth and purpose are two powerful guiding forces in our lives. Veritas is a story for readers of all ages and imparts wisdom that will help positively transform anyone's journey through relationships, teamwork, growth, and development."

— Amy P. Kelly, GPHR, SPHR, SHRM-SCP | VP of Consulting for The Jon Gordon Companies and author of G.L.U.E.

"Ali's life journeys are beautifully shared in a masterful encapsulation of the wisdom he has gained and wants to share with everyone. A meaningful and easy read, applicable for all ages. The only reason it took me more than an hour to read is that I constantly found myself reflecting upon and memorizing lessons that I want to apply in my daily life while inspiring others to do the same."

— Carl DiNicola | Ernst & Young Partner Emeritus

"The VERITAS principles are what every team needs to define what excellence looks like in their program. Each principle is clearly presented and gives a team the autonomy to discover their personal road map to their goals.

I highly recommend this training program and will continue to use it with my team every year."

— Michelle Winkler | PGA, Head Women's Golf Coach Cal State University, Northridge

"Ali has taken his wisdom and turned it into a simple yet powerful fable that teaches us the keys to a fulfilling life!"

— Max Rooke | Success Coach, Life 2 The Max, and Associate Head Women's Soccer Coach Pepperdine University

"VERITAS gives a thoughtful roadmap to apply right now to your journey. Don't wait!!! Use it again and again as new challenges forge you into your best self."

— Brett Bissell | Husband & Father, Founder of CFP Luminate Wealth Management

"VERITAS delivers a heartfelt story that inspires me to keep digging for who I could be. Ali captures the essence of these seven 'truths' with a tale that transcends a mere story of father and son."

"Ali has put together a group of 7 principles that have the power to change team culture. Through the course of our meetings, I saw our team grow to be more intentional on the field and in relationships with each other. We were challenged to be honest and vulnerable with ourselves, and each other, and we have learned skills to help us continue to do so. I am grateful for this program and its impact on our team."

VERITAS

7 Truths that Lead to a Purposeful Life

Ali Malaekeh

STREAMLINE
BOOKS

To all who are seeking their true purpose.

Contents

Introduction

The seven truths of VERITAS are universal and applicable in every walk of life regardless if you are a teenager, in your 70s, an aspiring professional athlete, a scientist, or a teacher. Finding your purpose in life and living a fulfilling life is for everyone.

VERITAS is a story about a father sharing seven truths with his son so that the son can pursue his dream of being a professional athlete.

I chose to write this story about a father and son because I always dreamed of having a son and sharing the sort of life lessons that Tobias shares with AJ.

I wish I could say I learned all seven truths from my father, but I learned these truths through my years of coaching and training in leadership development and mental performance. I have not stopped sharing them . . . with my beautiful bride Karen, my amazing step-daughters Chelsea and Malia, my niece Malak and great nieces Cici and Yaya, with the players I have coached, with coaches and athletes I meet with regularly, and with my friends. VERITAS is something we all need, and when we embrace it, it's life-changing.

May this fable be the catalyst that helps you start your journey toward finding your purpose, and equips and empowers you to live a fulfilling life.

Part One

Chapter 1

The Question

Tobias looked at his three-year-old son in awe. He never thought his dream of raising a son would ever be a reality. He had made so many father-son plans before AJ was born. Some of them had already become true: AJ falling asleep on his chest, Tobias seeing him take his first steps.

And there were so many dreams Tobias was looking forward to happening: playing catch with AJ, going to ball games with him, and having father-son talks when they grabbed lunch at the local In-N-Out.

"Daddy . . . why is the sky blue?"

"Daddy . . . why is the ladybug red and black?"

"Daddy . . . why . . ."

AJ was curious the way every three-year-old is curious. He wanted answers and he didn't give up until he got one. "I don't know" was never good enough. Tobias wasn't sure if AJ understood all his answers, but he always made the time to address his questions.

Tobias knew to cherish this. Time seemed to fly by, and he wanted to be present for AJ. He knew what an impact a present father makes in his son's life. He wanted to be there for AJ at every step of his journey and into adulthood. He had committed not to miss the milestones. And he couldn't wait for AJ to ask him *the question* that would propel him to live a purposeful and fulfilling life.

Tobias knew the day would come when AJ would ask him *the question*. He just had to be patient, because he knew that sharing the answer before AJ was ready would be a waste of time.

Chapter 2

Opening Day

AJ had looked forward to this day for years! It was his thirteenth birthday. He was officially going to be a teenager. But this birthday would be different. His dad had flown them to Chicago to watch their first Cubs game at Wrigley Field! AJ and Tobias spent a lot of time watching Cubs games on TV. It was *their* time. Living in California, they went to games in San Diego, Los Angeles, Anaheim, San Francisco, and Seattle. But AJ's dream was always to walk through the turnstiles of Wrigley Field and watch the Cubs play on their home turf.

Walking up to Wrigley Field was an experience in itself. Thousands of people streamed down the streets of Chicago, all headed to the greatest ballpark ever built. The closer they got to the ballpark, the crazier things became. People looking to buy tickets, people trying to sell tickets, souvenir stands on the corner of every street, food trucks.

And there it was—the big marquee:

Wrigley Field, Home of the Chicago Cubs, Welcome to Opening Day.

Tobias walked AJ around the ballpark to show him the statues of all the Cubs icons. Ferguson Jenkins, Billy Williams, Ernie Banks, Ron Santo. Tobias and AJ stopped at every statue, and as AJ admired them, Tobias gave his son a brief history of their accomplishments.

After they saw everything they needed to see, they got in line and walked through the turnstiles. AJ's heart was beating so hard he was sure everybody could see it through his shirt. As they walked through the dark walkway toward the field, he heard the crack of the bat. The smell of hot dogs, nachos, and popcorn couldn't steal his attention from the light ahead. In a few steps, he'd see the field and all the players.

They emerged onto the stands and there was the field in its grandeur. AJ's eyes locked on the Cubs in the middle of batting practice. The noise of the crowd was a background hum as AJ and Tobias walked down the steps toward their seats.

As AJ scanned the scenery, his eyes were drawn to a flagpole on the left of the scoreboard.

"Dad, what do the numbers on those flags mean?"

"Those are the jersey numbers of some of the great Cubs players," Tobias answered. "When players achieve greatness in their careers and they retire, teams can show their appreciation to the player by retiring their number. Number 23 is Ryan Sandberg's number, the great second baseman, and 31 is Fergie Jenkins and Greg Maddux's number, two of the greatest Cubs pitchers of all time."

AJ's eyes were glued to the flags as he headed toward the Cubs dugout. Tobias knew what AJ was thinking and was itching for AJ to ask him the question. Tobias didn't want to start the inevitable talk until AJ was ready. It was just a matter of time.

Chapter 3

It's Time

lmost three years after their father-son day at Wrigley Field, AJ walked into his father's office.

"Dad?"

Tobias immediately recognized the tone in his son's voice. As a 16-year-old high school junior, AJ never felt uncomfortable asking for help. Tobias gave him his undivided attention.

"What's up, AJ?"

"Dad, I love playing baseball. I love watching baseball. I love thinking about baseball. I want to be the best. I know you have helped so many of your players and friends go after their dreams. Can you help me?"

This was the day Tobias had been waiting for. AJ wanted to know how he could pursue his dreams. Tobias's 40-year journey as an athlete and coach had prepared him for this very day. He had helped countless people pursue their dreams and watched them thrive in the process. As rewarding as those experiences were, none would be better than helping his own son.

"I would love to help you achieve your dreams, AJ! Over the years, I have learned what it takes to live a purposeful life. I want to be honest with you. It's going to take some time to go through all the steps. It's a pretty simple process—but it won't be easy! Are you willing to commit to the process of what it takes to be the best?"

AJ's eyes lit up. He had witnessed the impact his dad's process had on so many people's lives—his players, assistant coaches, and friends—and how thankful they were for the process. Now it was his turn.

"Can we start right now?" AJ said.

Part Two

"The only thing worse than being blind is having sight but no vision."

— Hellen Keller

Chapter 4

Vision

"The first step in the process has five parts that you must go through in order."

"Sounds great! What's part one?"

Tobias waited a moment before he started speaking. He could sense AJ's anticipation.

"What's your *vision* for your future?" Tobias asked.

"I just want to be the best." AJ replied.

"That's all fine and dandy, but being the best looks like something. I know how much you love photography. What do you do when you want to take a picture of something that is far away?"

"That's easy! I zoom in on the object."

"That's exactly what you need to do with your dream. Look through your imaginary telephoto zoom lens that has the power to look into the future and take a close look at your dream. What does being the best baseball player look like? Who are you going to play for? What position are you going to play? Be as detailed as possible. Once you have that figured out, write it down, and then we can take the next step!"

AJ ran to his room, jumped on his beanbag, grabbed his imaginary camera, and started looking into his future, dreaming of exactly what his dream looked like.

He could see it: the Major League Baseball All-Star Game in Chicago—and he was the only Cubs player selected that year. He could barely hear the announcer over the roar of the crowd. *Starting at second base, representing the Chicago Cubs for the tenth time in the All-Star game . . .*

AJ started zooming into his stats, too. He dreamt of being a career .316 hitter and averaging twenty-two home runs a year over the twelve years he was going to play for the Cubs. He was going to play stellar defense and the six Gold Gloves were proof of that.

AJ sprinted downstairs and showed everything he had written down to his dad.

"That's awesome, AJ! I love how detailed your dream is. Whenever you look at it—and I would encourage you to do so often—don't be afraid to add more details to it. Before you take off on any journey in life, you have to start with the end in mind!

"Now you are ready for part two: *why.*"

AJ was confused. "What do you mean, *why?*"

Tobias knew this would make AJ dig down and think.

"Why do you want that dream? Your 'why' is such an important question because it will pull you toward your goal. We all face hurdles in our lives and so will you. Maybe your coach won't play you. You might get injured, or you may not get drafted in the first round—you know what I mean? Your 'why' is like a bungee cord. It pulls you over and through every obstacle in front of you toward your goal. Without a strong 'why', most people don't give 100 percent effort and they often change plans as soon as things get tough.

"The goal is to have a 'why' that is powerful and gives you the best chance to make your dream a reality."

AJ took a deep breath. "So you are saying that if I don't know why I want to play for the Cubs in the All-Star Game, then it's easy to quit on my dream when things aren't going my way. But if I know my 'why', I will be able to grind through the tough times."

"Exactly."

"What's your 'why', Dad?"

Tobias leaned back, took a deep breath as he pondered how best to share his 'why'. It involved a pivotal moment in Tobias's life. Everything had changed that day.

"I was going through a tough time a few years before I met your mom, and I reached out to my friend Kenny for some advice. He is the one who pointed me toward my ultimate purpose. That's when my life radically changed. Kenny took me under his wing and helped me become who I am today. He impacted my life so much, I wanted to do the same. So my 'why' is to inspire others to discover their purpose and empower them to live fulfilling lives. That's what keeps me going every day. Everything I do, I do through that lens. I want everybody to experience what I experienced."

AJ stared out the living room window, deep in thought.

"I think I know my 'why'. Remember when we went to Wrigley Field for my thirteenth birthday? After we made it to our seats during batting practice, while I was standing by the dugout hoping to get an autograph, Ben Zobrist came up to me and asked me how I was doing. I was speechless, Dad! Ben Zobrist, my favorite Cub, was asking me how I was doing! He wanted to know if I played baseball. When I told him I wanted to be a professional just like him, he told me never to give up on my dreams. He signed my jersey and gave me a ball. That moment was the best thing that has ever happened to me, and I want to be able to do the same for some kid one day. I want them to know that they can dream big, too."

"Love it, AJ! You have thought this through. Can you put your 'why' in a sentence that you can remember?"

AJ thought about it for a few seconds and said, "Inspiring and guiding athletes to pursue their dreams. How is that, Dad?"

Tobias was in awe of how quickly AJ formulated his thoughts. He didn't have to give AJ any of the advice he gave his assistant coaches and athletes when he took them through the process.

"Next, step three, you have to put a date on your dream. When do you want this to happen? You see, AJ, a dream will always stay a dream if you don't put a date on it. When you put a date on the dream, it comes to life and becomes a goal. When you put a deadline on your goal, you're going to be inspired to do what it takes to achieve your goal."

AJ did the math in his head. He was sixteen years old, and he wanted to play in ten All-Star games in the Majors. If he made it to the majors when he was twenty-four and played in his first All-

Star game when he was twenty-six, his tenth All-Star Game would be in . . .

"Dad, I figured it out—it will take me twenty years to reach my goal."

"That's right! Now it's a goal. The next step in the process is you have to plan out the next twenty years. But I am going to challenge you to do things a bit differently. Don't plan out the journey from today going forward. Plan it backwards and live it forwards."

"That sounds cool, but I don't know if I really get it."

"Your goal is twenty years away. What do you need to accomplish in ten years to put yourself on track to achieve your goals in twenty years? After you figure that out, figure out what you need to achieve in five years. Then figure out what you need to achieve in one year, then six months, one month, a week, and finally, tomorrow. Then, live it out forward, day by day. You want to make sure that your first step and every step you take after that is intentional and leads you to your goal."

"That's going to take some time to figure out."

VERITAS

"Absolutely, it is. One thing I've learned is to hold the plan with open hands, because things will happen that are out of your control, and you may have to change course while still pursuing your goal.

"As soon as you know your steps, you need to answer another tough question: Who do you need to be to reach your goals?"

"How can I be anyone other than myself, Dad?"

Tobias smiled as he thought back on his own journey.

"Let me give you an example. When I started my new career a few years ago, I questioned myself a lot. Am I good enough? Am I too old? Would people listen to me? I was allowing negative thoughts to affect my confidence. And I realized that I needed to be courageous and confident. So I started reminding myself of that every day and anytime I had doubts. Remembering who I needed to be helped me launch my new career.

"So identify one to three core principles that you are going to commit to living by so you can give yourself the best chance of achieving your goals."

"How can I pick these core principles?"

Tobias walked over to his desk and grabbed a sheet of paper. "Here is a list of potential principles you can choose. It's not comprehensive. You can come up with your own. Pick five that jump off the page. Then narrow it down to three and start living your life according to those three principles."

AJ looked over the list and started circling certain words, crossing off others. He finally picked his three words: disciplined, passionate, and thankful.

Tobias loved the words AJ picked, but he was curious why AJ had picked those words.

"Well, I picked *disciplined* because if I want to reach my goals, I can't take shortcuts. I picked *passionate* because I love baseball so much and I don't ever want to forget that. It's really what drives me. And I picked *thankful* for a lot of reasons. I am thankful for baseball, I am thankful for being good enough to compete, I am thankful for the opportunity to play every day—I can go on and on. I never want to forget how thankful I am!"

"AJ, I have been waiting for this day since you were born. I am so excited for you and I want you to know how proud I am of you! I am sure you are going to have questions, and I want you to know that I am always here for you."

"Excellence is not a singular act; it's a habit. You are what you repeatedly do."

— Will Durant

Chapter 5

Excellence

It took AJ two weeks to finalize the five steps Tobias had asked him to put on paper.

"Dad, I'm ready for the next step. I know what I want, I know why I want it, I know when I want to reach my goals, I built the path to my goals backward and want to start living it forward—and I know who I need to be to reach my goals."

"Awesome, AJ! It's time to start your journey. Remember when you were in second grade and your teacher, Miss Moore, would hand back your tests and homework? You'd run through the front door, waving the papers at your mom and me, wanting us to see what she wrote. Do you remember what she said on those assignments?"

AJ thought back. Miss Moore was his favorite teacher. He remembered looking forward to school, always paying attention, doing his home-work, and studying for every test. He remem-bered how excited he was when he saw what Miss Moore had written beside his grade.

"Yeah, Dad. She wrote, 'Excellent!'"

"And that is how you need to start approaching everything you do—with *excellence*. Remember, it's not about perfection, because perfection isn't possible. But when you do things with excel-lence, you are doing them to the best of your ability. You are 100% committed. If it's easy, do it with excellence. If it's hard, do it with excel-lence. If it's boring, do it with excellence. If it's one of those days that you have 70% in the tank, give 100% of what you have—and that is doing things with excellence. *Excellence* is about your commitment to the work that you need to do. When you do things with excellence, you are on the right road to pursuing your goal."

"I get it! I can't just go through the motions."

"Exactly! When you look at great athletes, CEOs, artists, and musicians, they have one thing in common: They made excellence a habit. Ask yourself, what does excellence look like in batting practice, in your infield practices, in your pre-game preparations, in your nutrition, in weight training, in school, in relationships. Look in every area of your life and develop habits of excellence."

"How can I make living with excellence an everyday thing?" AJ asked.

"You have to build habits that lead you to live with excellence. To start your day with excellence, start it with a win. Develop a great morning habit. This is what I do: when the alarm goes off in the morning, I open my eyes, put my feet on the floor, and walk across the room to turn my alarm off. Getting out of bed at the time I had planned is starting the day with excellence. If the alarm clock was by my bed and I had pressed snooze, I would have compromised on my wake-up time and I wouldn't have started my day with excellence. Next, I remind myself of three things that I am thankful for and drink a full glass of water before I go downstairs to grab my cup of coffee. Then I sit down and start reading. When I first started doing this, it was a bit of a struggle, but I stuck with it and now I can't imagine starting my day any other way."

"That makes sense. If I develop a bunch of habits that help me be my best, then they're helping me live a life of excellence. And when I live a life of excellence, it helps me chase after my goals."

"You got it, AJ! The goal is to see how many days in a row you can keep the habit going. And when you miss a day, don't beat yourself up. Just start another streak of days and try to beat the last streak. You can make a game of it. So here is your homework: make a list of all the things you want to do with excellence and then pick *one* thing. Focus on that one habit, make it part of your DNA, and then move to the next."

"Trust is the glue of life. It's the most essential ingredient in effective communication. It's the foundational principle that holds all relationships."

— Stephen Covey

Chapter 6

Relationships

As Tobias and AJ watched their favorite college baseball team compete in the opening round of the Big West Conference games, Tobias began to talk about the third truth.

"AJ, I have a question for you."

"What's up, Dad?"

"Do you think you can reach your goal by yourself?"

"For sure!"

"Really? You don't think you need the support of your mom and me? How about your coaches? How about your hitting coach? Your teammates?

Your strength coach? Your mental performance coach? Your friends?"

AJ started chuckling. "Okay, Dad! I get it! I can't do it alone."

"Other people will be on this journey with you—which means you need to learn the importance of *relationships* and how you can build them."

AJ was curious about how to develop the kind of relationship his dad was talking about.

"Think about your closest relationships. What makes them special?"

AJ's mind went into overdrive. He had close relationships with his family and a few of his teammates. For each relationship, there was one thing that they had in common, a special connection that drew them into a deeper relationship with each other.

"I can be who I am in all of my closest relationships. I can be honest about how I feel. I feel safe. I trust them and they can trust me."

"That's right, AJ. The common trait of all great relationships is trust. And developing that kind of trust is a process. How did you and Roger become such good friends?"

"We met playing baseball, and we started hanging out and talking about all kinds of things we were interested in. It was fun getting to know each other."

Tobias nodded. "People who trust each other hang out and talk with each other. They talk about all kinds of things. Things they have in common, life experiences, their dreams. They enjoy each other's company because they communicate well with each other. Not only is it easy to share what's on your heart, but you also enjoy listening to the person. And once trust is built, you develop a sense of commitment to each other."

"What do you mean, Dad?"

"When you develop a committed relationship, you feel safe sharing almost everything with that person. You might share things you are struggling with right now or even some past hurts from your life. You know you can trust them because of your shared commitment to the friendship."

AJ realized his friendship with Roger had grown to be what it was because they had taken the time to open up with each other. Trust was the foundation of their commitment to being best friends.

"Dad, based on what you are saying, I'm assuming you have that kind of relationship with your friend Jeff, right? You guys love to hang out, and when you are sitting in the back- yard, it looks like you are having some deep conversations."

"That's right. Jeff is one of my best friends. We can talk about anything and everything. He knows that I will always be there for him, and I know that he will always be there for me."

AJ started thinking of Jeff and his dad's friend- ship. Whenever Jeff called needing something, Tobias would jump at the opportunity to help him. And it worked the other way too. They celebrated events together and supported each other during tough times. Jeff came to the hospital when Tobias had knee surgery and went out of his way to make sure he was taken care of. He was checking in on him daily.

"You and Jeff are all in with your friendship!"

"That's right. We are committed to our friend- ship. We make each other better and help each other reach our goals. We treat each other the way we want to be treated and we are always honest with each other."

"That makes sense, Dad. Treating others the way you want to be treated will definitely build trust —and when you trust someone, you will do anything for them."

"You got it, AJ. We can't do life alone. We are made to be in relationships, and there is nothing more important than being in healthy relationships, helping and inspiring each other to grow. That applies to all of your relationships."

"Integrity is doing the right thing even when no one is looking."

— C.S. Lewis

Chapter 7

Integrity

"Dad, I cracked the screen on my phone. Can you take me to get it fixed?"

Tobias wasn't too happy about the cost of fixing the screen, but he was excited to spend the afternoon with AJ. They would have some quality father-son time driving to the Apple Store, waiting for the screen to get fixed, and driving back home.

"How did the screen break?"

"You won't believe it, Dad. I was recording myself in the batting cage so I could send the video to my hitting coach, when the ball flicked off the tip of my bat and shot right into the screen."

"Can you use it at all?"

"I can take calls. But it's hard to text and I can't really see anything on the screen. It's mostly useless when it's broken."

Tobias knew this was the perfect time to teach AJ about the fourth truth, *integrity*.

"When anything cracks, it lacks integrity. And anything that doesn't have integrity loses value and functionality."

"Where are you going with this?" AJ knew his dad was about to drop some wisdom.

"The Latin root for integrity is *integritatem*, which alludes to wholeness. If something lacks integrity, it's not whole. Your phone, with the cracked screen, lacks integrity. It's not whole, it's broken. This is the same when we talk about someone's character. If a person doesn't walk his talk, he lacks integrity. He's saying one thing and doing something else.

"Integrity is all about a person's character. A person with integrity is trustworthy because whatever they say, they do. When they say they're going to work hard, they work hard. When they say they're going to be a good team-mate, nothing will stop them from being a good teammate. They walk the talk. Do you know anybody like that on your team?"

AJ could think of a lot of people on his team who didn't have integrity. Teammates said they were going to work hard and didn't. Coaches said they cared about the player's development, but all they did was point out what players did wrong, instead of showing how to do something correctly.

"I can think of a lot of people who don't have integrity," AJ said with a chuckle.

"How do they make you feel?"

"Like I can't trust them."

"How about someone who *does* have integrity? There has to be someone on your team!"

"Well, Coach Tony has integrity. He says that he wants to develop us and he is always trying to help us learn. And he says that he is always there for us if we have questions. . . . When I asked him a question, he made time for me. I feel like I can trust him. And Roger, too. He's so honest!

The other day, the guy at Chipotle gave him an extra $5 in change. When he realized it, he made the 10-minute walk back to return the $5! He said the money wasn't his and he didn't want the other guy to get in trouble."

Tobias was excited that AJ knew the difference between having integrity and not having integrity *and* that he trusted and valued a person with integrity more.

"It's simple but not easy to have integrity. We know what is right, but sometimes we're put in positions where our integrity is at risk. Regardless of the situation, it's our choice to always speak the truth and follow through on everything we say. That way, we can be relied on as someone who's honest and trustworthy.

"It's never too late to start being a person of integrity. I haven't shared this with you, but when I was younger, I wasn't the most trustworthy person. I made some poor decisions and lied to get myself out of trouble. I got to the point where people didn't trust me, and that's when Grandpa Manley sat me down and told me about kintsugi."

AJ looked at Tobias as if he were speaking a different language. "Dad, first of all, I never knew that about you! I would have never guessed. Everyone trusts you. And what did Grandpa Manley talk to you about? Kin—what?"

"Kintsugi! It's the Japanese art of repairing broken pottery with a lacquer that is mixed with gold and silver. The potter 'glues' the broken pottery with the metallic lacquer and the value of the pottery goes up! The potter takes what was broken and makes it more precious. The same can be done with our character."

"So you're saying that if we make bad decisions, it doesn't ruin us for good."

"Exactly. I had to make a lot of apologies and earn back the trust that I had broken, but in time, some of those relationships grew to be stronger than I could have ever dreamed of. Unfortunately, I lost some friendships too. When I look back, the cost of losing those friendships was not worth it. Be a man of your word, AJ, and you will become a person who can be depended on."

"There is only one way to eat an elephant: a bite at a time."

— Desmond Tutu

Chapter 8

Trust the Process

AJ was frustrated. His batting average was dropping. Hitting below .200 was not part of his plan, and he was starting to worry that he'd lose playing time and college coaches and pro scouts wouldn't be interested in him anymore.

The weight of the pressure was getting to AJ. He wasn't being his usual self at home. When the family ate together, AJ was quiet. The sound of laughter was absent. When AJ got ready for practice, he didn't run out of the house with a smile on his face. He wasn't racing to get to practice because he loved baseball and being with his team so much.

Tobias knew AJ well and as a concerned father he had to step in.

"Are you okay, AJ? You haven't been yourself lately."

"Not really, Dad. I'm struggling. I am so worried about striking out. It feels like the pitches are coming at me at 110 miles per hour! And when I do get the bat on the ball, it goes straight to one of their players. They don't even have to move. My coach is probably going to stop playing me, and I think my teammates don't trust me anymore. It feels like I have an infectious disease —everyone is keeping their distance from me. It's miserable!"

"AJ, let me ask you this, didn't your hitting coach adjust your swing?"

"Yeah. He told me if I make a few small adjustments, I'm going to be able to see the ball better and hit it all over the field. I made the adjustments, but they're hurting my batting average."

"How did you feel when you first made the adjustments in the batting cages?"

"It was hard at first. Even though it was a couple of small adjustments, it felt different. I struggled the first couple of days. And then things slowly started to get better."

Tobias could hear a bit of hope in AJ's voice.

"So when you were in the cage, it took you some time to get used to the changes—but eventually you got comfortable with it. What were you focusing on?"

"I focused on opening my stance, where I was holding the bat and my hip rotation."

"Did you expect things to change right away?"

Tobias saw the spark in AJ's eyes.

"No, I knew it was going to take some time. And all I was supposed to do was focus on the details. . . . I get it!"

Tobias couldn't be prouder to see AJ grasp the next step.

"You have to *trust the process*. Getting from where you are to where you want to be is a journey. It's going to take time. And you have to be patient and focus on the things you can control. When you step into the batter box, you can control what you think and what you do. You have no control over the pitcher, the umpire, and how the other team is going to play defense. If you focus on what you can control and *trust the process*, you are giving yourself a chance to become the best version of yourself."

"You know what that reminds me of, Dad? When I started lifting weights. I could barely do a pull-up. My first real one took a lot of hard work. I had to keep doing everything my strength coach told me to do until I finally did one pull-up. It took a long time, but it felt so good when I finally could do them!"

"It's the same thing with your hitting and anything else in life, AJ. Just trust the process. Be patient, show up, and focus on the things you can control. That will remove a lot of pressure so you can perform at your best!"

"The first step toward change is awareness. The second step is acceptance."

— Nathaniel Branden

Chapter 9

Awareness

"**D**ad, do you mind if I go over to Trenton's to play some video games later? We're in the middle of the most epic tournament."

Tobias approved of all of AJ's friends. They each had a good head on their shoulders, played baseball together, ran in the same circle of friends, and enjoyed clean fun. He was only concerned about AJ being aware of how his activities with his friends would affect his dream.

"No problem, AJ. Before you leave, let me know when you have some free time on your hands. It's time for step six."

"Absolutely! How about right now?"

Tobias couldn't contain his smile.

"When I say *awareness*, what do you think of?"

AJ nibbled his lower lip, deep in thought. "I think of baseball. Before I step into the batter's box, I look at how the other team is set up defensively and remind myself about the pitcher's tendencies so I can be more ready for whatever he throws."

"That's a great example. How about outside of baseball?"

AJ had never thought of how awareness may be affecting his life away from the diamond. He couldn't come up with a good answer. "I'm not sure, Dad. But I'm ready to hear about it."

"When it comes to awareness there are two areas to focus on: inward and outward. Inward awareness is all about knowing yourself well. It's having a detailed scouting report on yourself. We need to know the things that we do well and the things that we can improve on. When you choose to be honest with yourself and operate from a place of self-awareness, you are going to be on the path toward your goals.

"Let's say you strike out on a pitch that bounces two feet in front of the plate. As you walk back to the dugout, are you aware of your body language? What are your thoughts? How do you feel? You see, if you're not aware of how you react, you're going to start slipping into a mindset that won't prepare you for your at-bat —and it may even affect your game when you pick up your glove and set up at second base.

"Then, there is external awareness. Do you know what landmines are, AJ?"

"Not really."

"Landmines are used during times of war to slow down or stop the opposing forces from advancing. They are explosive devices, hidden just under the surface of the ground, designed to blow up when someone steps on them.

"There are landmines in your daily life that may stop or slow you down from achieving what you want to achieve. Distractions are just like land-mines. If you are not careful, they can derail you from your mission."

"That makes sense, but I just don't see how it affects me."

"Baseball season is long. I know you're feeling the grind. You want to go to Trenton's house to play a video game. Now, there is no problem with that. But let me ask you this question: are you just going there so you don't have to do something you need to do, like work out or do your homework? If you are on top of everything and want to spend time with your friends having fun, that's all right! But if you are going to use video games to avoid the things you need to do to pursue your goal, take a step back. *Awareness* is about being aware of anything and everything that is going to slow you down or keep you from achieving your goals."

AJ's mind was spinning. He had never really taken the time to think about awareness and now that he was, he could see how his lack of awareness of the small things could and was affecting his journey.

"Thanks, Dad! I love hanging out with Trenton, but I have so much on my plate right now. We have a game tomorrow, and I didn't want to look at the scouting report Coach Tony sent me about the pitcher we're facing. I'll make sure to do that before I go!"

"There you go! Awareness is key to your goals. I spend about 10 minutes each day taking an honest look at myself and how my day went so I can be aware of anything that is slowing my progress toward my goals and make any adjustments I need to make. It's better to catch things early so you can stay on course."

"Great achievement is usually born of great sacrifice, and is never the result of selfishness."

— Napoleon Hill

Chapter 10

Sacrifice

Tobias was sitting in the stands enjoying the moment. It was the bottom of the ninth inning, no outs, runners on first and second base with the score all tied up. AJ was up to bat and Tobias knew the opposing pitcher didn't want to walk the bases loaded with Thomas, the hottest hitter on the team coming up next.

As the pitcher prepared his delivery to home plate, AJ squared up to bunt. He laid the perfect bunt down the third base line, moving the runners to second and third base. Then, it was Thomas's turn at the plate. He hit a deep fly ball to center field, allowing Nate to score the game-winning run.

Tobias waited for AJ after the game with a huge smile on his face. The smile wasn't only about the win that ensured the series sweep against their rivals. And it wasn't about the home run AJ hit. It was about how AJ helped his team win— and the opportunity Tobias now had to share the final truth with AJ.

He gave AJ a big hug and told him how much he loved watching him play and how proud he was of him. That always put a smile on AJ's face, win or lose.

"What was going through your mind when you stepped up to bat?" Tobias asked as they walked to the car.

"Well, as soon as Woody reached first base, I knew it was my chance. Not going to lie, Dad, my first thought was I am going to drive the ball in the gap and get the winning hit. But before I stepped into the batter's box, I looked at Coach and he told me to lay down a bunt. At first, I was bummed. I felt he didn't trust me and wanted Thomas to get the hit. I laid down a perfect bunt, all the runners advanced, and the rest is history. Thomas came up, hit a fly ball to center, Nate scored easily—and we won!"

Tobias knew AJ's coach well. They had been friends for a long time, and Tobias had helped him in his journey of seeking the truth about being the best. So he asked AJ a loaded question.

"What did Coach say after the game?"

"First, he congratulated the team for winning the series. Then, I thought he was going to praise Thomas for the game-winning RBI or Finn for pitching so well, but he put the spotlight on me. He said that one of the major reasons we won was my bunt! If I hadn't executed it, the runners would not have advanced and Thomas's at-bat would have looked different."

"And what do they call that bunt?"

"Come on, Dad—it's a sacrifice bunt!"

They both started laughing as they climbed into the car. As soon as they quieted, Tobias shared the final truth with AJ.

"This is it, AJ. The last of the truths: *Sacrifice.* You experienced firsthand how sacrifice allowed the team to win and achieve your goal to sweep your rivals. To give ourselves the best chance to achieve what we want to achieve, we need to be able to sacrifice. Sometimes, we have to sacrifice our ego so the team wins. And the reality is, when the team wins, we win. Sometimes, we have to sacrifice doing things we want to do that are fun so that we give ourselves the best chance to be great.

"It goes hand in hand with being aware. When you are aware of where you want to go and the obstacles in your path, you have to be willing to sacrifice."

AJ nodded and leaned back in his seat, staring out the window.

"Do you remember what Grandpa Manley's favorite food was?"

"Bacon!" AJ said with a smile, remembering all the meals Grandpa Manley made with bacon.

"Remember when he received his medical report six months ago? The doctor told him he had to change his diet. So Grandpa Manley took a hard look at all he was eating and decided he had to cut out bacon from his diet. Do you know why he did it?"

"Yeah! He said it was important to him to live long enough to come to watch me play in college and the pros."

"That's it! He gave up something he enjoyed so he could have the chance to see you grow up and thrive."

AJ stared out the window as they pulled into their neighborhood. He turned to his dad and said, "Dad, I just want you to know that I am going to do everything in my power to live out what you have told me. I want to be the best second baseman when I make it to the pros. And I am going to apply the seven truths to every area that is important to me."

Tobias leaned back and smiled with pride as they pulled into the driveway.

"Can you remind me, AJ, what are the seven truths?"

"I need to have a *vision*, do everything with *excellence*, invest in the *relationships* in my life, have *integrity*, *trust the process*, be *aware*, and *sacrifice*," AJ said with confidence.

"Take the first letter of each of the seven truths —what does that spell?" Tobias asked.

AJ made mental notes as he went through the seven steps. "VERITAS?"

"You've got it," Tobias said, as they got out of the car. "VERITAS means *truth* in Latin. When you live out these seven truths, you're giving yourself the best chance for your goals to become reality."

THE END

Kind of . . .

Bonus Chapter

Finding my true purpose allowed me to discover the principles of VERITAS, leading me to live a truly fulfilling life. I alluded to that life-defining event in Chapter 4. The bonus chapter is about Tobias sharing that life-defining event with AJ. Just scan the QR code below, enter your email address and I will email you the PDF.

Action Plan

The principles of VERITAS can be used universally by anyone to pursue their dreams and passions because they are based on true principles. I have seen them work in my life and the lives of countless other people. The Action Plan is your guide to implementing the principles of VERITAS in your life.

If you have any questions, feel free email me at
ali@alimalaekeh.com

VISION

CHAPTER 4

AJ was a talented baseball player and passionate about it. He had a dream of being a MLB All-Star, but didn't know how to achieve this so he asked his father, Tobias, what he needed to do to make his dream come true. Tobias shared the first pillar of VERITAS with him.

Studies show that you are 1.2 to 1.4 times more likely to achieve your goals if you vividly describe them. Look into the future and "see" what it is that you want to accomplish based on your passions and gifts.

What: You will never get where you want to go if you don't know where you are going. Start with the end in mind. If there was something you could do and failure was not an option, what would it be? Write down your dream in as much detail as you can.

_____

_____

_____

_____

_____

_____

_____

_____

_____

_____

_____

_____

Why: Your "why" is the bungee cord that ties you to your dream. What is the "why" behind your dream? Why do you want to make the dream a reality?

_____

_____

_____

_____

_____

_____

_____

_____

_____

_____

_____

_____

When: Let's turn the dream into a goal. A dream becomes a goal when you put a timeline on it. When do you want to accomplish your goal?

_____

_____

How: Plan out your journey to your goal. If your dream is to become reality in ten years, what is your five-year plan? How about your three-year plan? What do you want to achieve in one year? How about ninety days? Do you have a plan for the next thirty days? One week? Tomorrow? Build your journey from the end backwards to today, and live it out daily. Take a look at your goals and your journey at the beginning of each week to propel you forward and at the end of your week to plan out the next week and make any necessary adjustments.

Who: Who do you need to be to give yourself the best chance of making your dream come true? First, look over the list on the next page and put a checkmark beside any word that stirs something in your heart. Then, go back and circle the ones you feel most strongly about. Then narrow it down to one to three words.

Accountable	Excellent	Optimistic
Adventurous	Experienced	Original
Authentic	Fair	Passionate
Aware	Faith	Peaceful
Balanced	Flexible	Professional
Beauty	Focused	Resilient
Bold	Free	Respectful
Calm	Friendship	Responsible
Committed	Fun	Selfless
Compassionate	Generous	Sensitive
Confident	Grit	Simple
Connected	Growth-minded	Sincere
Conscious	Healthy	Structured
Content	Honest	Supporting
Cooperative	Hopeful	Sympathetic
Courageous	Humble	Thankful
Creative	Influential	Thoughtful
Decisive	Integrity	Timely
Determined	Joyful	Trusting
Dependable	Kind	Understanding
Diligent	Leader	Unique
Disciplined	Loving	Useful
Educated	Loyal	Virtuous
Effective	Mindful	Visionary
Empathetic	Motivated	Warm
Encouraging	Open	Wisdom

<u>EXCELLENCE</u>
C**HAPTER** 5

Tobias knew the dangers that AJ faced now that he had a clear vision. He needed AJ to know that it is not about perfection but excellence, always giving what you have to achieve the goal that you want to achieve. And excellence starts with habits.

Establishing key habits that help you pursue your goals is essential to living a life of excellence.

Morning Routine: How do you choose to start your day? Some ideas: gratitude journal, reading, drinking 18 ounces of water, making your bed before you leave your bedroom.

_____
_____
_____
_____
_____

Nighttime Routine: How do you end your day? You could . . . pick out your clothes for the next day, review your day and celebrate wins, identify one thing you could have done differently and plan to address it, turn all electronics off one to two hours before bedtime, and stretch.

_____

_____

_____

_____

_____

RELATIONSHIPS
CHAPTER 6

Tobias reminded AJ that his journey to the MLB All-Star games is not one that he can go on alone. A lot of people will be part of the journey. Tobias emphasized the importance of having authentic relationships.

What are the key relationships in your personal life?

_____
_____
_____
_____
_____

What are the key relationships in your work life?

_____
_____
_____
_____
_____

Who do you need to meet with intentionally this week to build a stronger relationship with them? Think about some questions you can ask to get to know them better.

_____

_____

_____

_____

_____

_____

_____

_____

_____

Remember: healthy communication leads to commitment and trust.

<u>INTEGRITY</u>

CHAPTER 7

AJ needed his phone repaired and Tobias saw the perfect opportunity to share the importance of a person's character. Integrity is the foundation of one's character and if there are any cracks in it, they must be addressed in order to win people's trust.

Review the last thirty days of your life. Have you kept your word? Have you consistently given full effort at practice/school/work?

_____

_____

_____

_____

_____

_____

_____

_____

_____

_____

_____

Identify the cracks in your character—even the small ones—and make a plan to address them on a personal level and have conversations with others, if needed (apologize, take responsibility, etc.)

_____
_____
_____
_____
_____
_____
_____
_____
_____
_____
_____

<u>TRUST THE PROCESS</u>
CHAPTER 8

The journey to your goal is going to take time, and it's not always going to be easy. Tobias reminded AJ that he has to trust the process and not change course or get frustrated quickly. AJ's focus needs to be on what he can do today so that he can get a step closer to what he wants to accomplish in the future.

In your quest to reach your goals, are you focusing on the next "bite" of the elephant? Are you feeling overwhelmed with the tasks at hand? Does your goal seem too distant?

You can only control what happens right now. What is the next step you can address today that will inch you closer to your goals?

_____

_____

_____

_____

_____

Action Plan

AWARENESS

CHAPTER 9

As a coach, Tobias knew about the importance of continually assessing the progress of your team, as well as scouting your opponents. Tobias takes the opportunity to share the importance of self-awareness, not only about his strengths and weaknesses but also about things that may be slowing AJ's progress to his goal.

It's time to write a scouting report on yourself. You must be 100% honest.

Inward Inventory: What are your greatest strengths? What are the areas in your life where you need to grow the most? When you identify the areas in your life that you need to grow the most, pick one and make a plan to address it.

_____

_____

_____

_____

_____

79

Outward Inventory: In your day-to-day life, what is keeping you from being fully committed to pursuing your goals?

<u>SACRIFICE</u>

CHAPTER *10*

AJ's sacrifice bunt was important for the team's victory. Tobias used the opportunity to tell AJ about the importance of sacrificing things so that he could continue on his journey to his goals.

There are a lot of good things you can do every day. Sometimes, those good things get in the way of excellent things. What good things do you have to say "no" to so you can say "yes" to the excellent?

Action Plan

Sacrifice and selflessness go hand in hand. Who can you affirm this week in front of others?

Thank You

This fable is a collection of lessons I have learned along my life journey. I am thankful for all the people who have intentionally invested in my life. I am thankful for all the people who have mentored me from a distance—through books, podcasts, and seminars. This project would not have come to fruition without you.

Kenny Luck, thank you for pointing me to the ultimate truth.

Jon Gordon, thank you for your wisdom and guidance. I could probably write a book about how all your books have impacted my life. Thank you for allowing me to serve on your team and share the importance of positive leadership wherever I go.

Max Rooke, thank you for your continued friendship and encouragement. Thank you for walking me through the adventure of Good to

Great. The journey gave me the confidence to step into a space I never thought I belonged.

Brian Cain, you ignited a love of mental performance in me that I never knew existed. Your Mental Performance Mastery certification has allowed me to walk alongside so many people, helping them be the best version of themselves.

Bob Wilson, thank you for believing in me and igniting my heart's love of leadership and character development.

Tony Colavecchia, you saw something in me that no one else saw. You gave me an opportunity to play soccer for you and then you invited me to serve as your assistant coach, changing the trajectory of my life. Thank you for believing and investing in me.

Adam Goodman, thank you for giving me the platform to step into the lives of coaches and athletes, propelling me to where I am today.

Kris Gibbs, Ireland Walton, and Nate Green thank you for reading this fable and help making it what it is today.

Last but not least, my amazing and beautiful bride Karen, thank you for loving me and encouraging me every day to pursue my purpose. I am blessed to call you my bride.

BRING THE POWER OF *VERITAS* TO YOUR ORGANIZATION

KEYNOTES

WORKSHOPS

CONSULTING & COACHING

Visit https://www.alimalaekeh.com/ or email ali@alimalaekeh.com for more information.